We hope that you enjoy this
Early Soundplay story
again, and again, and again!

Children love repetition. It helps them build their
knowledge and understanding of word meanings and
story structure. Children also love sound play – it's fun!
And it helps develop their ability to recognise and say
speech sounds in different words. These are key foundation
skills for success in phonics, early reading and spelling.

This story is full of sound play with a special focus on 's'
and 'r'. The simple, interactive storyline makes it easy for
children to anticipate what happens next and to join in
when they hear the story again. This provides lots of
opportunities for them to both hear and practise saying
's' and 'r' words.

Reading stories and looking at picture books together is one
of the best ways in which you can support children's spoken
and written language development.

B000 000 021 5038

D1439840

ABERDEEN LIBRARIES

Clickety Books Ltd
Victoria Beacon Place, Roche, Cornwall PL26 8LG, UK

All rights reserved. No part of this publication may be
reproduced, stored in a retrieval system, or transmitted, in
any form, or by any means, without the prior permission of
Clickety Books Ltd.

Illustrations ©Clickety Books Ltd 2015
Text ©Clickety Books Ltd 2015

First published by Clickety Books Ltd 2015

ISBN 978-1-907968-35-8

Printed and bound by Short Run Press Ltd
Exeter EX2 7LW, UK

www.clicketybooks.co.uk

Sally the Sea Lion

Written by Sally Bates

Illustrated by Sarah-Leigh Wills

Series Editor Anne Ayre

Some things to look out for...

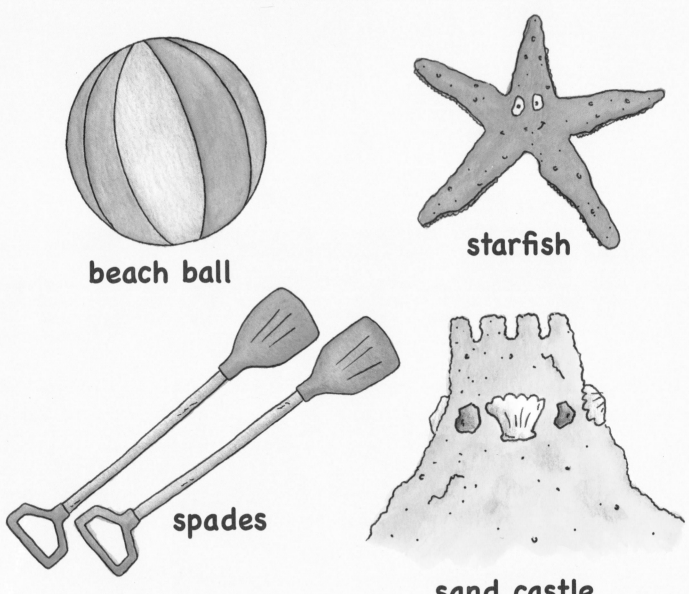

beach ball

starfish

spades

sand castle

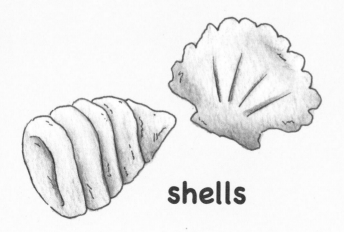

shells

book

sun shade

buckets

Sally the Sea Lion is looking
for her best friend Ryan.
Sally and Ryan are playing hide and seek
and it is Ryan's turn to hide.
Shall we help Sally look for him?

Sally the Sea Lion sees...
yellow sand and blue sea,
seagulls, sailing boats...

sun shades, buckets and spades.
But Sally the Sea Lion can't see Ryan.
Can you see him?

Sally the Sea Lion sees...
Suki scooping sand to make a castle.

But Sally the Sea Lion can't see Ryan. Can you see him?

Sally the Sea Lion sees...
Bessie and Bella
bouncing beach balls.

But Sally the Sea Lion
can't see Ryan.
Can you see him?

Sally the Sea Lion sees...
Ross, Reece and Rufus
racing and chasing each other.

But Sally the Sea Lion
can't see Ryan.
Can you see him?

Sally the Sea Lion sees...
Ruth and Ruben reading by a rock pool,
a bright orange starfish, silver sea shells and...
a grumpy red crab.

But Sally the Sea Lion
can't see Ryan.
Can you see him?

Sally the Sea Lion sees...
Riaz and Rosie wriggling into rubber rings.
But Sally the Sea Lion can't see Ryan.
Can you see him?

Sally the Sea Lion sees...
Nora and her little daughter Dora
dressing up in sea weed, sun glasses
and purple spotty swim shorts.

But Sally the Sea Lion can't see Ryan.
Can you see him?

Sally the Sea Lion sees...
Stella skimming stones.

'Stop, Stella, stop!' says Sally the Sea Lion
'I can see Ryan! I can see Ryan!'
Can you see him?

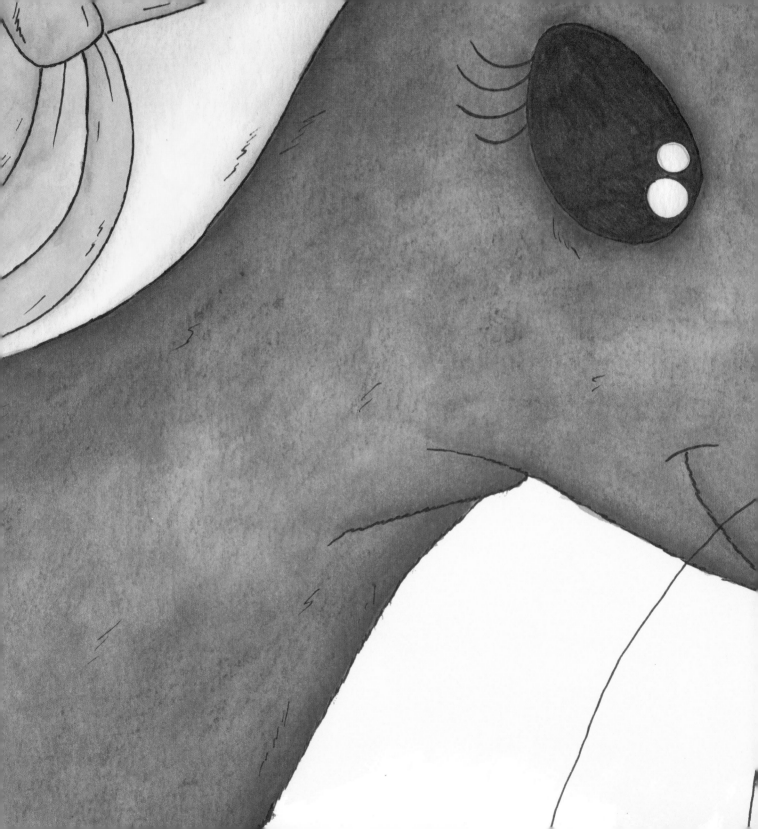

Sally the Sea Lion
has found Ryan!

Now it is Sally the Sea Lion's turn to hide.

And it is Ryan's turn to look for Sally.

Ryan sees...
Suki, Bessie and Bella, Ross, Reece and Rufus,
Ruth and Ruben, Riaz and Rosie,
Nora and her little daughter Dora.

But he can't see Sally.
Can you see her?

Did you spot Sally's special 's' and 'r' words?

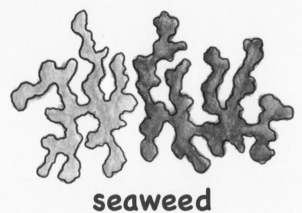

seaweed

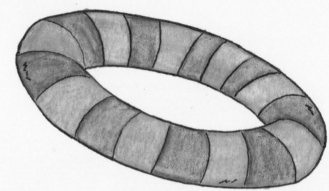

rubber ring

ryan

sun hat

red crab

sun glasses

seagulls

sailing boat

More fun with Early Soundplay...

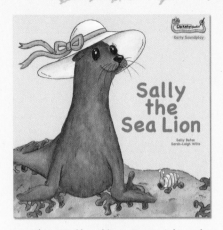

Look! Sally the Sea Lion is playing hide and seek on the beach with her best friend Ryan. Sally can't see Ryan anywhere. Can you see him?

Join Tess and Bess as they squeak and squeal having lots of fun in the snow! They go skating, sledging, snowballing and make a big snow-mouse.

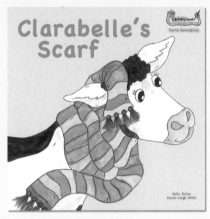

It's cold on the cliffs. Clarabelle the calf has lost her scarf. She shivers and sniffs then giggles and laughs when she sees who's taken her scarf.

Chatty Bat loves to chitter chatter chat with everyone. It's very noisy with constant chatter until it's time to sleep – then no more chatter, not a peep!

Join Clip Clop and her friends Hip Hop the bunny, Yip Yap the puppy and Flip Flap the bird as they set off for a picnic. Clip clop, clippety clop.

Jake the snake likes baking cakes. Yummy scrummy cakes! However, he is a bit of a silly snake and ends up with a tummy ache.